Mary Middleton-Dutson
3537 E Pueblo Avenue
Mesa, AZ 85204

# HOW ARE YOU FEELING TODAY?

Designed by Bill Foster of Albarella & Associates, Inc.

Distributed to schools and libraries
in the United States by
ENCYCLOPAEDIA BRITANNICA EDUCATIONAL CORP.
310 South Michigan Ave.
Chicago, Illinois 60604

Library of Congress Cataloging-in-Publication Data

Perry, Susan, 1950-
How are you feeling today? / written by Susan Perry;
illustrated by Anastasia Mitchell
p. cm.
Summary: Discusses various aspects of mental health,
including self-perception, mental illness, emotional
problems, and getting help.
ISBN 0-89565-876-3
1. Mental health — Juvenile literature. 2. Emotions —
Juvenile literature. [1. Mental health.]
I. Mitchell, Anastasia. ill. II. Title.
RA790.P375   1992
616.89 — dc20                          91-46589
                                       CIP
                                       AC

# HOW ARE YOU FEELING TODAY?

Written by Susan Perry

Illustrated by Anastasia Mitchell

THE CHILD'S WORLD

## FEELINGS

How are you feeling today? Are you feeling happy or sad? Confident or worried? Lonely or accepted and liked?

Every day each of us experiences many different feelings. Some feelings are comfortable – like love, acceptance, confidence, happiness, pride, and security. These feelings make you feel good about yourself and about the people around you.

Other feelings are uncomfortable. Such as anger, defeat, disappointment, fear, grief, worry, jealousy, and loneliness. These feelings can make you feel bad about yourself and about the people around you.

Uncomfortable feelings are the ones you feel when you get emotionally upset. It's okay to get upset from time to time. Everyone does. It's part of everyday life. It just means you are reacting to a temporary stress or problem in your life.

ARGHHH!

GULP!

Getting emotionally upset is a lot like having a cold. A cold can make you feel uncomfortable or even angry, but you know that everyone gets colds and that yours will soon end. You also know that you'll get a lot more colds during your lifetime.

It's the same with emotional upsets. From time to time, you may feel angry, worried, or depressed. But these feelings usually last a short time and disappear.

Sometimes, though, uncomfortable feelings last for a long time, maybe even weeks. You may feel them very strongly – so strongly that they affect your overall behavior and thoughts. Now it's no longer an upset feeling you're experiencing, but an actual mental or emotional illness.

## A HEALTHY OUTLOOK

To understand how and why people get sick with things like colds and flus, doctors must first understand how a healthy body works.

It's the same with mental illness. The best way to understand mental illness is by first understanding what it means to be mentally healthy.

Mental health has to do with how we feel about ourselves, how we get along with other people, and how we meet the demands of life. Sometimes our mental health is good and sometimes it's not so good. Good mental health is happiness, peace of mind, enjoyment, satisfaction – all those comfortable feelings. Good mental health is something we all want for ourselves, although we may not call it that.

People who are mentally healthy can usually:

- Cope with their emotions
- Take life's disappointments in stride
- Deal with most situations that come their way
- Accept responsibilities
- Welcome new experiences and new ideas
- Think for themselves and make their own decisions
- Get satisfaction out of doing things
- Give love and consideration to other people
- Set realistic goals for themselves
- Laugh at themselves
- Like and trust other people and expect that other people will like and trust them

There are a lot of other traits that could be added to this list. Can you think of some?

Of course, not everybody has all the traits of good mental health at one time. No one is that perfect. And, of course, just knowing what good mental health is doesn't mean you can go out and be mentally healthy. But it can help you think more clearly about it.

## TAKING STOCK OF YOURSELF

Good mental health begins with feeling good about yourself. How are you feeling about yourself today?

- Do you feel you are smart?
- Do you feel important?
- Do you try to make others feel special?
- Do you like the way you look?
- Do you feel others like you?
- Are you a fun person to be with?
- Do you try to be nice to people who are not popular?
- Do you feel like you get along well in school?
- Are you able to laugh when you make a mistake?
- Do you have fun?

When you think about your answers, do you think you feel good about yourself? Are there any answers you wish were different? What could you do to change?

## WHAT IS MENTAL ILLNESS?

A mental illness is a lot like a physical illness. It has a cause. It upsets your system and makes it act differently than usual. And it needs care and treatment for recovery.

Having a mental illness does not mean you're "crazy." It just means that you are unable to cope with the daily tensions of life. You feel overwhelmed with those uncomfortable feelings of fear, anger, distrust, and depression.

Mental and emotional illnesses are common. About one in seven Americans – or 32 million people – suffer from mental or emotional

THAT'S ALOT OF PEOPLE!

SURE IS!

problems that are serious enough to need professional help.

Here are some other facts about mental illness:

🐾 One out of four hospital beds in the United States are occupied by people with mental illnesses

🐾 One out of 10 people in the United States will be hospitalized for mental illness during his or her lifetime

🐾 About 60 percent of the people who complain to their doctors about being sick have an emotional problem that is responsible for their sickness

🐾 Mental illness costs Americans about $37 **billion** each year

Mental illness is America's number one social problem.

## WHAT CAUSES MENTAL ILLNESS?

No one knows for sure what causes mental illness. It may be caused by chemical changes in the body. Or it may be caused by our reaction to things that happen to us. Or it may be caused by events that happened a long time ago and which we thought we had forgotten.

There are some warning signs for mental illness. One sign is a constant feeling that something bad is going to happen when there is no real reason for worry. Another sign is a bad case of the "blues" – so bad that you don't care what's going on around you. A sudden and dramatic change in mood or behavior can also be a warning sign. And feeling sick when you aren't really sick can be a symptom too.

## HOW TO PICK YOURSELF UP WHEN YOU'RE FEELING DOWN

Everybody has uncomfortable feelings from time to time. These feelings – or tensions – are often good for us because they keep us on our toes. For example, being nervous during an exam or a soccer game can actually make you perform or play better. Too much tension, however, can make you miserable.

It's up to you to understand and deal with your feelings. Here are some things you can do when you're feeling tense or "down":

## TALK IT OUT

Explain your feelings or problem to someone you trust. Talking about a problem will make you feel better – and it might help you find a solution.

BLAH! BLAH! BLAH!

## BE WITH PEOPLE

Don't pout and keep to yourself. Do things with your friends or family. Or make new friends by joining a club or starting a new activity.

## BE NICE TO YOURSELF

Instead of thinking about all the things you don't like about yourself, try making a list of all the things you do like. You may find that you're a lot nicer than you think.

## TAKE ONE STEP AT A TIME

Don't try to change everything in your life all at once. Pick one small thing you'd like to change and do that first.

## GET RID OF ANGER

Bottled up anger may explode and hurt you and other people. Find a way to let go of anger. Remember, it's okay to cry, scream, yell, or hit or kick things that cannot be damaged – as long as you don't hurt or bother anyone else while you're doing it.

## DO SOMETHING FOR SOMEONE ELSE

Helping someone else will make you feel more self-confident and better about yourself. (And it will make the person you're helping feel better, too.)

It's not easy to do these things when you're feeling upset. But you should give them a try.

## WHEN BAD THINGS HAPPEN

Have you ever suddenly gotten very sick? Or have you ever had a cold that turned into something more serious, like strep throat or maybe even pneumonia?

The same thing can happen with your feelings. You may be feeling okay or just a little bit "down" and then something painful happens that makes you really depressed. The pain may be so great that you think you'll never be happy again.

Lots of things can cause that pain: the death of someone you love, your parents getting a divorce, maybe even a move to a new house and school.

These kinds of events happen to all of us at some time in our lives. It's normal to be very depressed about them. No matter how much hurt you're feeling, however, remember that the pain will eventually go away even if you think it never will.

## HOW TO PICK SOMEONE ELSE UP WHEN HE OR SHE IS FEELING DOWN

If someone you know is emotionally upset, there are some things you can do and some things you should not do to help that person feel better.

Let the person know you care. People with emotional problems often feel like they are all alone in the world.

WE LOVE YOU!

Be a good listener. People with emotional problems often just need someone to talk to about their problems.

See if there is some way you can help ease the person's problem. Maybe, for example, a friend is really upset because his or her grades aren't very good. Perhaps you could find a way to help your friend study better.

Don't judge someone who has an emotional problem. Don't call that person names like "selfish" or "weak" or "mean." That may only make the person believe even more strongly that everyone is out to get him or her.

Don't argue with someone who has an emotional problem. You can't convince a troubled person that what he or she is doing is wrong.

Don't blame yourself for someone else's emotional problems. You are not responsible for the way other people act.

## GETTING HELP

Just like everyone gets colds, everyone experiences uncomfortable feelings from time to time. It's okay to have these feelings. They are a normal part of everyday life.

Sometimes our uncomfortable feelings become so strong that we may actually experience an emotional or mental illness. Then we need to get some help.

If you think you or someone you care about has a mental or emotional illness, find someone you trust to talk to about your feelings. Here are some people you might want to talk with: your parent or parents, a teacher, a doctor, a nurse, your religious leader, a social worker, a school counselor, or a friend. Or you could call your local mental health treatment center. Just look in the phone book under "mental health."

Don't be ashamed or embarrassed to ask someone for help. Getting help can bring back those comfortable feelings and make you feel better about yourself. Then, when someone asks you, "How are you feeling today?," you'll be able to answer: "Great!"